A SOLVE-THE-STORY PUZZLE ADVENTURE

PUZZLOO!ES

MYSTERY AT MALLARD MANSION

D1313796

BY RUSSELL GINNS AND JONATHAN MAIER
ILLUSTRATED BY KRISTEN TERRANA-HOLLIS

Copyright © 2021 by Random House Children's Books

All rights reserved. Published in the United States by Random House Children's Books, a division of Penguin Random House LLC, New York.

Random House and the colophon are registered trademarks of Penguin Random House LLC.

Visit us on the web! **rhcbooks.com**
For a variety of teaching tools, educators and librarians can visit us at **RHTeachersLibrarians.com**.

Library of Congress Control Number: 2020948206
ISBN: 978-0-525-57205-3 (trade paperback)

Cover design by Igor Jovicic
Cover art and interior illustration by Kristen Terrana-Hollis
Interior design by Peter Leonardo

Printed in the United States of America

10 9 8 7 6 5 4 3 2 1

First Edition

Random House Children's Books supports the First Amendment and celebrates the right to read.

What's a Puzzlooey?

Puzzlooies are stories you read by solving puzzles.

They're smart, surprising, and seriously silly.

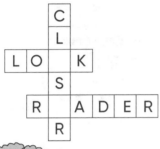

Each amazing adventure is chock-full of challenges, perplexing pictures, and mysterious messages. Plus there's always an extra helping of hilarious jokes and fascinating facts!

Let these zany brainy kids introduce you to the story. They might even help with a clue or two. Start reading and puzzling. It's all up to you!

Eunice   **Maralee**

Ray   **Clinton**

How to Solve This Story

DETAIL DETECTOR

Every Puzzlooey is told through a mix of chapters and puzzles. To solve it all, you'll have to pay attention to things you've discovered along the way.

CLUE COLLECTOR

PUZZLES ARE...

A-MAZE-ING!

You'll need a few things to make the most of this book:
- A pencil
- Scissors
- A ruler

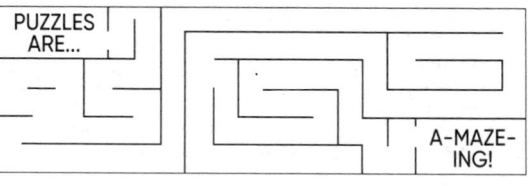

PUZZLER PROPS

* READ THE FIRST LETTER OF EACH BOLDED WORD

Most of all, you'll need to use your **Bagpipe Radio and Invisible Notebook Sandwich***

(Psst: Don't skip ahead before solving a puzzle.)

Quack the Case!

You're just in time for a crime. This Puzzlooey is filled with secrets, sleuthing, and a stolen trophy.

It's an **eggshell**-ent tale about a celebrity duck, some dastardly wrongdoing, and a detective discovering who done it. You'll need to pause and **pond**-er to solve the puzzles. So be careful, because you never know **waddle** happen next.

Settle into your nest and don't rest until the crook has confessed.

Here comes the...

MYSTERY AT MALLARD MANSION

 U

U R 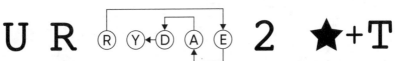 **2**

A DEAD DUCK

My phone rang at 7 a.m. on Saturday. I muted the T.V.

"Detective Stanley Dench here," I answered. "Who's interrupting my cartoons and Frosted Crunchies?"

"Marvin Mallard," said the caller. "Know me?"

I knew him. *Everybody* knew him. Marvin Mallard was the world's most famous movie star and celebrity duck.

"Oh, Mr. Mallard," I said. "I loved you in *Quack to the Future*. I thought your acting was really—"

"I don't have time for flattery," Mallard squawked. "Someone has stolen my Egg."

"Egg?" I asked. "You have a baby?"

"No!" Mallard snapped. "It's a trophy. It's my Golden Goose Egg Lifetime Achievement Award. I only had it for one day, and now it's missing. Find the thief!"

"I'm sure I can crack it," I said.

"My Egg?" he asked.

"No, sorry," I replied. "I'm sure I can crack *the case*."

"I'm counting on it," said Mallard. "Now bring your featherless butt over to my mansion right now!"

The line went dead. I didn't know it then, but it wouldn't be the only thing that died that day.

Mallard Mansion stood high on a hilltop. From the outside, it looked like your typical rich movie star's home with a gurgling duck fountain in the yard.

The knocker on the front door was shaped like a webbed foot. I gave the door a couple of loud raps.

When no one answered, I pressed the door buzzer. I heard music from the Mallard movie *Feathers of Fury* blaring inside the house.

Minutes passed.

I was just about to look for another entrance when the massive door slowly creaked open.

There stood the Wizard of Waddles, the Prince of Poultry, and the King of Quacks. It was Marvin Mallard himself. He wore a silk robe and a pair of enormous slippers on his big webbed feet.

"Hello, Mr. Mallard," I said. "I'm Detective Dench, remember? You needed my assistance with..."

Mallard didn't look at me. In fact, he didn't seem to be focused on anything at all. His eyes gazed off in two different directions.

"Mr. Mallard?" I asked. "Are you okay?"

He swayed back and forth. Then he opened his bill and tried to speak:

"Loose...goose..."

THUD!

He fell flat on his face.

I spotted a giant lump on the back of his head.

Suddenly, I heard footsteps.

"Here's your breakfast, Mr. Mallard," a voice called.

A bearded man in a chef's hat stepped into the entrance hall.

The man carried a serving tray piled high with torn bits of bread and what looked like a glass of murky green water. When he spotted Mallard, he dropped the tray.

CLANG! CRASH!

Bread chunks, water, and broken glass splattered across the floor.

"Oh, dear!" said the man. "What happened?"

I knelt down next to Mallard and felt for a pulse.

Nothing.

"He's a...dead duck," I said. "Somebody played knock-knock on his noggin. And I'm going to find out who did it."

I looked up at the man.

"Who are you?" I asked.

"I'm Ballotine," he answered. "I am—*I was*—Mr. Mallard's personal chef."

I thought about Mallard's last words: "Loose...goose."

What was Mallard trying to tell me? Was it about his Golden Goose Egg award? I already knew about that.

"Where did he keep his award for lifetime achievement?" I asked Ballotine.

"I'm not sure," he replied. "I stay in my kitchen. But I suppose you could look for it in the trophy room."

"Show me," I said.

As we passed through a hallway full of framed letters, Ballotine said, "Messages from Mr. Mallard's friends."
I read a few to see what I could learn.

1   ZOO WHO?

Each of these messages contains the name of an animal. (The first one has been done for you.) Find them all to reveal what Mallard's "friends" really thought of him.

1. "No one is better at acting and dancing than you, Marvin."

2. "Keep ignoring what the critics say. All your movies are wonderful."

3. "I cannot believe it was you in that mask. *Unknown Duck* was a great movie."

4. "Thanks for inviting me to a delightful dinner at your mansion."

5. "Let's talk. Call me now or maybe tomorrow."

6. "The movie was fantastic. I'm in awe. A seldom seen triumph of acting genius!"

So, some people weren't really Mallard's "friends."

"Here's where he kept all his trophies," said Ballotine, as he opened a set of doors and walked away.

CRACK THE CASE

Find every trophy case that matches the shape of another case. Only one trophy case doesn't have a match—that's the one with the Golden Goose Egg award.

THE TROPHY ROOM

I found the trophy case with the Golden Goose Egg.
The award wasn't missing at all!

I leaned in to take a closer look.

One trophy should match the other.
On the right side, circle six things that don't match.

The Golden Goose Egg award had a big dent with a duck feather sticking out of it! Yes, it looked as if I'd found the murder weapon. But why steal a trophy just to deck a duck and then put it back?

I took out my phone and called the chief of police.

"Hi, Chief Armstrong," I said. "Marvin Mallard's dead. Send a team right over."

"Sorry," he replied. "Two knitting supply trucks just collided. Yarn everywhere. We'll be tied up for a while."

I sighed. It looked as if I was on my own.

Then, as I stepped out of the trophy room, I saw someone coming down the stairs. It was a woman in a sparkly purple outfit and a mask with a bird beak.

"Are you a burglar?"
I asked.

"Of course not,"
she answered. "I'm a
superhero!"

She looked at my
rumpled coat and hat.

"What are *you* supposed
to be?" she asked.

"A detective,"
I answered.

"I see," she replied. "Are
you pretending to be a
duck-tective?"

Long ago, Mallard starred in "World's Greatest *Duck*-
tective." I loved that show, but that's not why I was here.

"No," I told her. "I'm a *real* detective."

"And I'm *real* hungry," she said. "Where's breakfast?"

"Hold on," I said, "Mallard has been murdered."

"Marvin? Dead?" She gasped, taking off her mask.

I recognized her immediately. She was Carlotta
Zanetti, the famous director. She directed the movies
Fowl Force, *Fowl Force Two* and *Fowl Force Four*.

"A murder," she said. "Now I've lost my appetite."

"Where were you 15 minutes ago?" I asked.

"In the Superhero Suite," she said. "Flying."

"Flying?" I repeated. "Superhero Suite?"

"I'm dressed as a superhero," she explained. "I'm the
Purple Partridge."

Now it made sense: Mallard played the Webbed Foot Warrior in the *Fowl Force* movies, and the Purple Partridge was his partner.

"Show me this Superhero Suite, please," I said.

"I can," Zanetti replied. "But do you ever get airsick?"

"Why would that matter?" I asked.

"Oh, you'll see," she said. "Follow me up the stairs."

As we headed to the next floor, I realized that Mallard built his mansion as a tribute to himself. Every room featured a different part of his career.

"This place is like a museum," I said.

"No," Zanetti said. "More like an amusement park."

"And why are you here?" I asked her.

"Marvin invited some of his friends to stay over," she answered. "He wanted all of us to celebrate his big-deal lifetime achievement award."

"Sure," I said. "But did he really have any friends?"

Zanetti raised an eyebrow.

"You figured that out," she said. "Yes, Marvin was a mean bird. He paid me very little to direct his movies. As the Purple Partridge might say, 'He was *cheap, cheap, cheap, cheap.*' "

"So you killed him," I said.

Zanetti laughed, but she didn't answer.

We stopped at the top of the stairs in front of a doorway. A sign read SUPERHERO SUITE.

"Put this on," Zanetti said, handing me a costume. "You can be the Phantom Flamingo."

"What?" I asked. "Why?"

"It's the only way into the suite," she answered.

She attached a long wire to her belt, then she held out a second wire.

"Here," she said. "Here's a line for you, too."

As soon as I was attached, the wires yanked us through the doorway and up into the air.

"The *Fowl Force* takes flight!" she announced.

"Aaaaiiiieeee!" I shouted.

We were both being flung around like a couple of cat toys.

"Tilt your head to steer," Zanetti said.

Find your way to the Superhero Suite. Start at the entrance. The correct path will lead you to a mask.

After I explored the suite, I turned to Zanetti.
"Okay," I said. "You couldn't have killed Mallard."
"How did you figure that out?" she asked.

5   NO ROOM FOR DOUBT

This word search is filled with everything Dench investigated. Find them all, forward, backward, and diagonally. The leftover letters spell out how he knew Zanetti was innocent.

```
T  E  L  E  V  I  S  I  O  N
E  P  S  P  H  G  T  S  E  K
E  C  U  L  U  R  N  I  C  S
P  B  A  R  I  C  I  N  A  E
N  H  P  L  S  P  R  K  L  D
I  E  O  T  K  E  P  E  P  C
G  W  S  N  D  C  R  E  E  L
H  O  T  A  E  W  E  A  R  O
T  D  E  L  C  R  G  N  I  S
S  N  R  P  E  T  N  S  F  E
T  I  S  W  S  E  I  T  I  T
A  W  A  L  P  L  F  U  W  T
N  R  O  R  R  I  M  A  S  A
D  A  P  E  T  O  N  R  M  H
```

LOOK HERE FOR LIST OF SEARCH WORDS ➤

SEARCH WORDS

CLOSET	NECKLACE	RUG
CUP	NIGHTSTAND	SINK
DESK	NOTEPAD	SLIPPERS
DRAWER	PEN	SUITCASE
FINGERPRINTS	PHONE	TELEVISION
FIREPLACE	PLANT	WINDOW
HAT	POSTERS	
MIRROR	PURSE	

"You're right. It wasn't me," Zanetti explained. "But I have a feeling that the killer was—"

Her wire yanked her up and out of the room!

Count each matching set of pictures.
If they have an odd number, cross them out. The letters on the remaining pictures spell what Dench discovered.

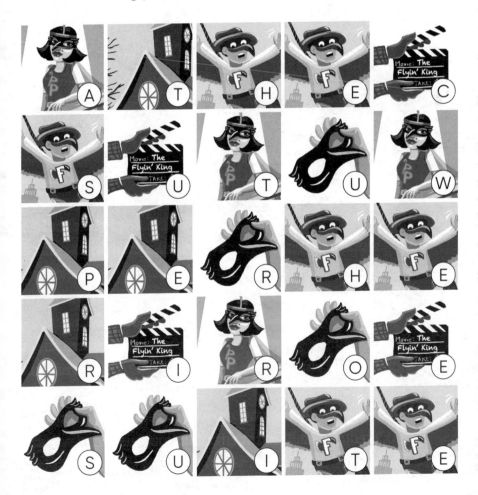

THE HALL OF ALL THE MUSICALS

Back at the doorway to the Superhero Suite, I found Carlotta Zanetti's flying wire. Somebody had snipped it. Where did she go?

As I took off my Phantom Flamingo outfit, I heard someone approaching. A small boy wearing yellow pajamas and thick glasses raced toward me.

In one hand he carried an electric shaver.

Strange, I thought, *The kid doesn't look old enough to shave.*

"I was in my room," he said. "I just heard a scream."

As he got closer, I realized this was no kid. Not only did he have a deep voice, but he had beard stubble on his chin.

"Carlotta Zanetti's flight was cut short," I told him, holding up the end of the wire.

"Is she okay?" he asked.

"I'll be sure to ask...when I find her," I said.

"Who are you?" the young-looking man asked.

"Detective Dench," I answered. "Who are *you*?"

"Don't you recognize me?" he replied.

He removed his glasses and thrust his face at mine. It didn't help. I still didn't recognize him.

"I'm Avi Babu," he sighed, putting on his glasses. I still didn't have a clue as to who he was.

"No one *ever* recognizes me," he groaned.

"Why should I?" I asked.

"Have you ever seen a Marvin Mallard movie where he has a son?" he replied. "Or a flashback where you see Marvin as a kid? Well, that's me. It's *always* me."

Babu waved his arms in the air. He was upset.

"I'm the world's oldest child actor," he continued. "But no one knows who I am. I'm always in duck makeup. And no one else hires me for anything else! 'Sorry, duck boy,' they say. 'Got no parts for ducklings. We'll give you a duck call when we need you.' "

"I get it," I said. "But tell me, how do you feel about Marvin Mallard?"

"I hope he *never* makes another movie," he replied.

"He won't, unless it's a ghost story." I said. "Mallard's been murdered."

"He what? How? When?" Babu stammered.

"Show me where you've been this morning," I said.

Babu led me to a red velvet curtain and stopped.

"I spent the morning strolling around in here," he said, pulling back the curtain.

A huge space shimmered with theater lights and colorful posters. A big flashing sign overhead said THE HALL OF ALL THE MUSICALS.

"I was in all these shows, too, you know," said Babu.

Speakers began blaring. It was a song from Mallard's hit musical *The Flyin' King*.

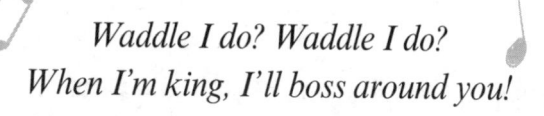

Waddle I do? Waddle I do?
When I'm king, I'll boss around you!

"I tried out for the part of the hyena," Babu shouted over the music. "That would have been great, but no! I got *Baby Duckling,* of course. I had to wear a diaper!"

The place was as vast as a shopping mall, but instead of stores, it had exhibits and rides all based on Mallard's musicals: *Beauty and the Beak, Duck Duck Moose, Nest Side Story, Flight School Musical,* and many others.

"This way," Babu said. "I'll show you exactly where I was this morning."

He led me to a photo booth at the *Princess and the Poultry* exhibit and handed me a photo.

"Look," he said. "That's me right there."

I examined all the details carefully. I could see a person in a costume with some props. The time stamped on the photo said 8 a.m. with today's date.

"The person in this picture is wearing a knight's helmet and armor," I said to Babu. "How do I know it's you?"

Fit all the items in Babu's photo into the crossword puzzle. The colored boxes will reveal what Dench found in the photo booth that proved Babu is telling the truth.

Armor	Castle	Flag	Shield
Banner	Cloak	Gloves	Spear
Belt	Feather	Helmet	Sword

"I left my bathrobe behind in the booth," Babu said. "That proves I was here. But, I bet you the killer is—"

Suddenly, a trap door opened, and he fell out of sight! I jumped in after him.

8 DOWN THE TUBES

There's only one way to reach the bottom of this maze of tubes. Help discover the HOLE truth.

I spilled out of the tube into a new room.

There was somebody waiting for me there, but it was definitely not Babu!

Create a picture of what Dench saw. For each pair of coordinates listed, draw the corresponding shape in the grid. For example, A9 has already been added.

■ = B8, C7, D3, D6, D7, D8, D9, D12, D13, E2, E4, E5, E7, E9, E11, E12, E13, F1, F2, F3, F4, F5, F7, F9, F10, F11, F12, F13, G2, G4, G5, G7, G9, G11, G12, G13, H3, H6, H7, H8, H9, H12, H13, I7, J8, K8, L7

◤ = A8, B7, C6, C13, D2, D5, G10, I3, K7

◣ = C3, E10, H2, H5, I6, I13, K6, M7

◸ = H4, K9, H10

◢ = B9, D4, D10, I8

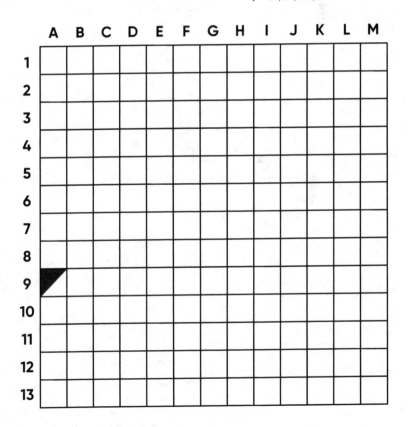

THE ASTRO LOUNGE

In front of me stood a robot with a ray gun.

"DO NOT MOVE," the thing said in an electronic voice. "I AM A RO-BOT WITH A RAY GUN."

Yep. My detective skills hadn't let me down.

"STATE YOUR NAME," the robot said.

"Dench," I answered. "I'm a detective, and I'm here to solve a crime. But who are you?"

"I TOLD YOU," it buzzed. "I'M A RO-BOT WITH A RAY GUN AND—*AH-CHOO*!"

"Do robots sneeze?" I wondered out loud.

"THERE, UM, IS A SHORT IN MY CIR-CUITS."

I glanced around the room. A sign above us said
ASTRO LOUNGE.

Model spaceships and planets hung from the ceiling. Dozens of screens displayed videos of space battles. Stuffed space creatures stared out from display cases.

Now it made sense. This room was dedicated to Mallard's sci-fi movies.

"STAY STILL," blared the robot. "OR I WILL BLAST YOU WITH MY DEADLY POWERFUL—"

I took a step forward and plucked the ray gun out of the robot's mechanical hand.

"THAT DOES NOT MATTER," it buzzed. "I CAN STILL FRY YOU WITH MY EYE-LASERS."

I pulled off the robot's head.

Inside was another head, belonging to a woman. Her face was flushed. It must have been hot in that costume.

"You got me, detective," the woman said.

Her voice sounded normal without the helmet's cheap microphone.

"The sneeze gave me away, didn't it?" she said. "I couldn't help it. There's gotta be ten year's worth of dust inside this suit."

"*Gesundheit*," I told her. "Now explain who you are, what you're doing inside a robot suit, and what you know about any murders."

"I'm Fran Flumpkin," she answered. "I came down to breakfast, and that's when I found out that Marvin was dead. I panicked and ran upstairs to hide."

"Let me guess," I said. "You worked for Mallard, and you hated him."

Flumpkin's eyes widened as if I'd just performed a magic trick.

"I was Marvin's agent," she said. "He came to me when his career was going nowhere. He could only get roles in cheesy low-budget horror films. Movies like *Count Drake-ula*, *Quackenstein*, and *Wing Kong*. Then I personally launched him to superstardom."

Her face hardened into a scowl. "But last night, after he'd won that Golden Goose Egg Award, he fired me! He said he didn't need me anymore."

"So," I said, pointing at her. "You used the trophy to give him one final *smash hit*."

"Nah," Flumpkin replied. "It couldn't have been me. I've got terrible aim."

She glanced around to make sure we were alone, then said, "But I bet I know who murdered Mallard. It was probably—"

"Wait!" I interrupted. "Every time somebody's just about to tell me who they think the murderer is, something happens and they disappear."

"Where am I going to go?" asked Flumpkin. "I'm stuck in a big metal robot costume. Nothing's going to happen to—"

R-R-R-RUMBLE!

The room shook. I lost my balance and fell to the floor.

Breep! Breep! Breep!

An alarm sounded, and I heard the voice of
Marvin Mallard!

"A long time ago, in a pond far, far away..."

It was a recording, of course. Probably the intro from
one of Mallard's science fiction films.

Ka-chunk! Squish! Squish! Ka-chunk!

A mob of robots and aliens charged into the room.
They waved glowing axes and other strange weapons.

"PRE-PARE TO BE DE-STROYED!" announced
one of the robots.

"I'm not a science fiction fan," I said.

"It doesn't matter!" cried Flumpkin. "Something triggered a scene from a movie, and we're trapped in it!"

10 MOVIE MAYHEM

Start at the top left arrow and read the letters as you go.
When you reach a new arrow, head in that direction.
The trail will spell the name of Mallard's famous space thriller.

START →	P	O	↓	W	→	P	↓
	L	→	N	Y	M	↓	I
	E	R	D	↑	E	S	R
	N	→	W	H	E	→	E
	↓	A	←	→	H	B	S
	→	R	S	T	↑	↑	T
	T	↓	E	K	I	R	←
	A	→	S	B	E	A	K

"Pond Wars! The Empire Strikes Beak!" Flumpkin shouted. "In the movie, there was a secret code to stop the evil *Death Wader* from destroying the galaxy!"

11 BATTLE OF THE BUTTONS

Find a row of four buttons that are all different shapes **and** are all different letters. Then find a column of four buttons that have all different letters and shapes too. Read all those buttons to find out how they can survive.

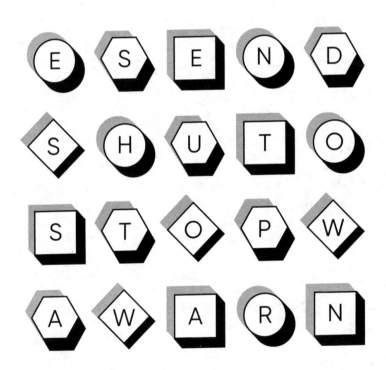

"Shut down!" I said as I tapped the buttons.
The robots and aliens stopped in their tracks. Lights
on their chest plates all began to flash the same message.

Cut out the square. Fold it four times (on the dotted lines) to make a smaller square that is blue on one side and gray on the other. The blue side will reveal the message on the robots.

A	P	☺	S	O	ロ	ᴚ	Ǝ
I	L	⌐	∀	O	W	⊥	Ǝ
U	W	⅄	ᴚ	O	⅄	∀	∪
U	☺					B	☺
N	!					Q	U
O	D					P	D
Y	E					☺	B
ᴚ	∀	Ɔ	☺	Ǝ	Ǝ	˥	O

The detective's fate will have to wait, while we take a break to educate ourselves with some...

Amazing Facts

The first detective story, "The Murders in the Rue Morgue," was written by Edgar Allan Poe in 1841. The bad guy turned out to be an orangutan!

Most ducks can fly by the time they are two months old.

A duck has a field of vision that's nearly 340 degrees. (360 degrees is a full circle.)

When mallard ducks snooze in groups, a guard duck sleeps with one eye open to watch for threats.

Ducks have three eyelids.

Eugène-François Vidocq is considered to be the first private detective. He was born in France in 1775.

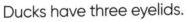

"The Big Duck" is a two-story building in Flanders, New York, that is shaped like—you guessed it—a duck!

The world record holder for the largest collection of rubber ducks has more than 9,000 of them.

Sherlock Holmes is the most popular fictional detective of all time. He's appeared in more than 300 books, movies, and TV shows.

A male duck is called a drake, a female duck a hen, and a baby duck a duckling.

Ducks are found on every continent except Antarctica.

Hawkshaw, gumshoe, and shamus are all words that mean "detective."

The smew, wigeon, and bufflehead are all types of ducks.

In 1976, the song *"Disco Duck"* became a No. 1 hit.

It wouldn't be an official, licensed, investigative, by-the-book Puzzlooey without...

Riddles and Jokes

Q: What has feathers and webbed feet and shakes buildings until they collapse?
A: An earth-*quack*!

Q: Where did they find the dirty, dusty detective?
A: At the scene of the grime.

Q: Why do ducks fly south for the winter?
A: It's too far to waddle.

Q: Why do ducks lay eggs?
A: The eggs would break if they dropped them.

Q: Why do ducks quack?
A: Because they can't oink or moo or bark.

Q: Who tracks down CROOK-odiles?
A: An investi-GATOR.

Q: Who caught the cr_m_nal?
A: Two private I's.

Q: Who stole the bathtub?
A: The *robber* ducky!

Q: What do you call a crate full of ducks?
A: A box of quackers.

Q: Who do ducks call when their keys don't work?
A: The *flock*-smith.

Q: What should ducks do before they fly south?
A: Check the national *feather* forecast.

"I bought my duck a pair of glasses. They weren't fancy, but they fit the bill."

We now return to
MYSTERY AT MALLARD MANSION

Knock-knock.
Who's there?
Quack!
Quack who?
Quack! Open the door and find out.

All at once, the robots and aliens turned toward the exit and zipped out of the Astro Lounge.

"You did it!" said Flumpkin.

Flumpkin's robot suit began to follow after them.

"Help!" she cried. "This costume is moving by itself!"

I ran after her into a hallway, but it was empty by the time I got there.

Across the hall was a small door. It looked different from every other door I'd seen in the mansion. It wasn't fancy at all. It was plain and smudged with dirt. Here and there, the door's brown paint had peeled away.

On the wall next to it, a sign read LI RA Y.

Some letters must have fallen off.

"Lipraky?" I puzzled out loud. "Licrazy? Lirraby?"
No. That's wasn't right. I used my detective skills...
"Library!" I exclaimed.

After flying around like a superhero and dodging robots, it felt good to be a private eye again.

I studied the faded logo on the door:

"Magazines and literature," I guessed and twisted the doorknob.

The door didn't budge.

"It's locked," said a voice.

To my right, I saw Chef Ballotine walking toward me down the hall.

"Mr. Mallard didn't like to read," he said with a snort. "He never went in there. I'm pretty sure it's just full of old furniture."

"Can I take a look inside?" I said.

"Go right ahead," Ballotine answered. "But I can't help you. I don't have a key. I've never been in there."

"Why are you up here anyway?" I asked. "The kitchen is downstairs."

"No one came to breakfast today, so I went looking for our guests," he answered. "But you're the first person I've seen. Is everyone all right?"

"If *everyone* includes Marvin Mallard, then no," I replied. "And everybody else keeps disappearing. I'd be careful if I were you."

Ballotine raised a hand as if taking a solemn vow and said, "I'll stay within the walls of my kitchen."

He bowed slightly and started to walk away but then stopped. He turned back with an eager smile on his face.

"Perhaps you would like to pause your detective work and have breakfast," he said. "I'm quite a good cook, you know. I've prepared an arugula-and-truffle omelette with a side of liver sausage, plus freshly baked croissants, gently squeezed orange juice, and a delicious—"

"No thanks," I said. "I had coffee this morning, plus a bowl of Frosted Crunchies."

Ballotine scowled.

"Fine," he snapped. "Then I'll be off. If you'd like to continue exploring, may I suggest the rooms around the corner? *Those* doors are open."

"Thanks for the tip, chef," I said. "Oh, and don't touch the duck. It's a crime scene."

"Hmph," Ballotine grunted. "Mr. Mallard always loved making a scene."

With that, he spun on his heel and headed downstairs.

When I was alone again, I pulled out a small leather case from my coat pocket. It contained my special set of lock picks. With these tiny tools and my skills, there wasn't a door lock that I couldn't open. I'd be in the library in no time.

I opened the case and–oops! Inside the case was chewing gum. I'd grabbed the wrong case that morning.

I was going to have to find another way into the library. I scanned my surroundings.

A few feet away, a portrait of Marvin Mallard hung on the wall. I took a closer look.

The painting had hinges on one side. When I pulled, it swung open like a door, revealing a rack of keys.

One of them *had* to open the library.

Use these clues to find the key to the library:
1) It is *below* a black key. 2) It is not a square key. 3) The key *to its left* is a different shape. 4) It has a number on it.

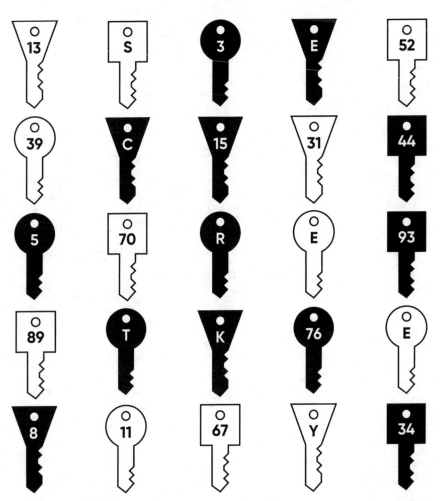

Everywhere I looked I saw old posters and flyers that advertised a variety act.

Now I knew what M&L actually stood for!

Tilt this page back until you can read one word.
Then turn it sideways, tilt it back, and read the second word.
You'll discover the meaning of "M&L."

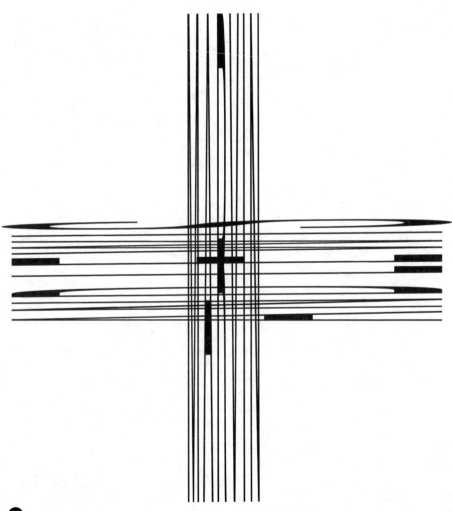

"Marvin and Lewis," I said, reading a poster.

But someone had spray-painted **X**s over Mallard's eyes and a sentence above his head.

To find out what was written on the poster, start at the "I" and read every fifth letter until there are no letters left.

START

I	E	O	N	H	T
D					B
E					U
H					M
V	E	L	E	S	A

THE ROOF

The library wasn't used for storing furniture. It was used to store old posters, photographs, and newspapers. Every single item was about Marvin & Lewis.

I scanned a few of the news articles.

Marvin Mallard and Lewis Ball were a popular entertainment duo, way back at the beginning of Mallard's career. One was a human, and the other was a duck. They sang and danced and told jokes. Audiences loved them. But when Hollywood called, Marvin left Lewis and became a movie star without him.

I knew then who'd murdered Mallard: his old partner! But where was Lewis Ball now?

Just then Chef Ballotine stumbled into the room.
His shirt sleeve was torn and blood spattered his face.
"Detective, come quack–I mean quick!" he cried.
"Somebody tried to grab me. I barely fought them off."

"Who was it?" I asked. "Where did they go?"

"I didn't get a good look," Ballotine gasped. "They
ran up the stairs to the roof. Marvin parks his hot air
balloon up there. Hurry! They're trying to escape."

I dashed down the hallway and raced up the stairs.

On the next floor, I found an exit and rushed outside
onto a wide, flat roof. The hot air balloon was tethered to
the building by a short rope. The big balloon was shaped
like a duck, of course.

I looked inside the balloon's basket. Nothing there.
I peeked over the edge of the building to see if there was
some other way to leave the roof and—*oof!*

Someone pushed me from behind, and I sailed into the air!

Unfortunately, I wasn't a duck. Zero feathers. Zero wings.

Fortunately, the mansion had eaves, dormers, turrets, a weather vane, flagpoles, chimneys, and frog-faced gargoyles.

Thump!

Bang!

Bonk!

As I fell, I hit every fancy architectural ornament, rolling off one, then hitting the next one and the next one and the next one.

Fump!

I landed in the arms of Chief Armstrong. Behind him stood a squad of police officers.

"We just got here, and I saw you taking a tumble," he said. "You okay?"

"Nice catch," I told him, rubbing a bruise on my elbow. "I'll get better, but Marvin Mallard won't."

Chef Ballotine came racing out of the mansion.

"The murderer!" he shouted. "The fiend is escaping!"

He pointed to the sky. The duck balloon rose high overhead.

"Don't worry." I said. "No one's in that balloon. The murderer is still here."

Look Closer!

This is it! It's up to you to solve one last puzzle.

To complete this challenge, you'll need to take a look back at some of the chapters and challenges you've solved along the way.

If you can do it, you'll discover who turned a famous feathered film star into an unlucky duck.

Chief Armstrong said, "Who, Dench? Who did in the duck?"

"The answer is staring us in the face," I said.

16 A BRILLIANT DE-DUCK-TION

Complete all the questions, then follow the dotted line. When you read the letters in order, you'll find out who murdered Marvin Mallard!

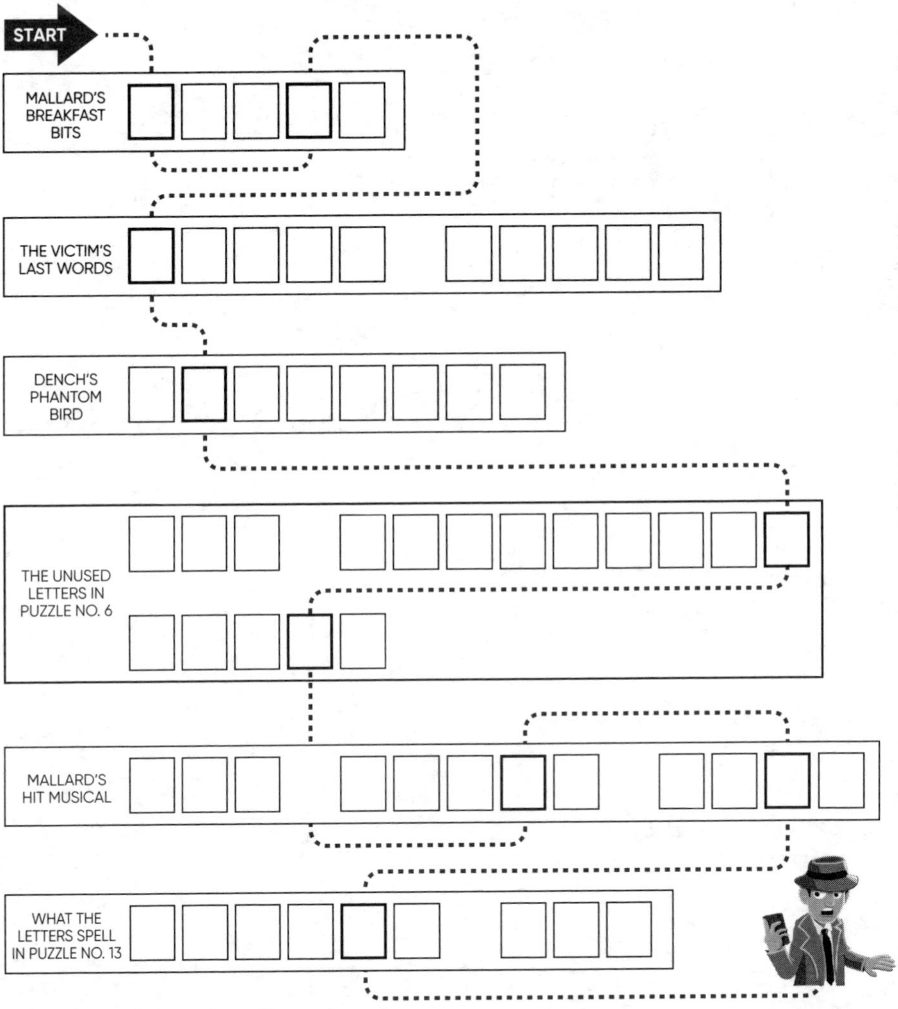

START

MALLARD'S
BREAKFAST
BITS

THE VICTIM'S
LAST WORDS

DENCH'S
PHANTOM
BIRD

THE UNUSED
LETTERS IN
PUZZLE NO. 6

MALLARD'S
HIT MUSICAL

WHAT THE
LETTERS SPELL
IN PUZZLE NO. 13

"That's ridiculous!" Ballotine said. "The real killer tried to beat me up!" He pointed at the blood on his face.

"One moment," I said. "Chief Armstrong, you can put me down now."

"Absolutely!" cried the chief, setting me on my feet.

I swiped some blood off Ballotine's face with my finger. I tasted it.

"Spaghetti sauce," I said. "Delicious."

"Why, thank you," Ballotine smiled, then caught himself. "Wait! No! I'm just the cook!"

"But you weren't always a cook," I said. "I didn't recognize you at first without the beard. And you were much younger in those posters."

"I don't know what you're talking about," said Ballotine.

"Moments before he died, Mallard told me exactly who killed him," I explained to Chief Armstrong. "He said, 'Loose...goose.' "

The chief looked confused. He was waiting to hear more.

"The 'goose' was the murder weapon, the Golden Goose Egg," I said. "But I didn't know what the 'loose' meant."

I looked over at Ballotine.

"Excuse me," I said. "What's your first name?"

Ballotine's eyes went wide, then he started to run.

"Stop him!" shouted Chief Armstrong.

Police officers swarmed in a circle around the chef.

"His first name is Lewis," I said. "Lewis Ballotine. He shortened it for his stage name, Lewis Ball."

Armstong nodded.

"Mallard wasn't saying 'loose,'" I continued. "He was saying '*Lewis.*'"

"You got nothing on me!" Ballotine said.

"Here's what I think happened, Chief," I explained. "Mallard left his old partner behind to become a movie star. Then I guess Marvin felt just a little bit guilty, so he hired Lewis as his personal chef.

"But all these years did nothing to take away Lewis's jealousy," I explained. "The lifetime achievement award was the last straw."

"Marvin called me to find his missing trophy," I said. "But by the time I got here, Lewis had already used it on his boss and then replaced it in its case. Mallard's so-called friends knew who Ballotine really was. But before they could warn me, he got rid of them."

"Rid?" Armstrong asked. "Are they dead, too?"

"Maybe," I answered. "Or maybe there's a place here where a mad chef can lock things away."

"A walk-in refrigerator!" said Armstrong. "Go, team!" Several officers rushed into the mansion.

"Ballotine tried to do me in, too," I continued. "He lured me to the roof. He planned to make everyone think the killer had escaped in the balloon. Isn't that right, Lewis?"

Lewis Ballotine exploded with anger.

"Before he met me, Marvin was a nobody!" he shouted. "He was performing in waterholes for frogs and geese. He was just a talentless, unknown duck!"

He couldn't stop. He was spilling the whole story.

"And *then* he makes me his chef," he continued. "But what does he like to eat? Chunks of bread and pond scum! My only job is ripping up stale bread every morning, noon, and night!"

Ballotine snatched the chef's hat off his head and threw it to the ground. "I should've been the star! *It should've been me.*"

"Cuff him," Armstrong said.

Ballotine didn't struggle as an officer handcuffed his arms behind his back. He just hung his head, defeated.

Soon, Zanetti, Babu, and Flumpkin shuffled out of the mansion. They were shivering but safe.

Together, we stood on the lawn and watched the duck balloon float away.

"Gee, Mallard was killed with his own lifetime achievement award. Makes you think, huh?" I said. "Poor duck, he never realized that being a good friend is a true lifetime achievement."

You Did It!

You reached the end of this Puzzlooey, and—quack! Wasn't that a whole flock of fun?

We couldn't have caught the culprit without your sleuthing skills, puzzling power, and detection perfection.

So stick a feather in your cap! Because of you, another lawbreaker has learned that crime doesn't pay.

Now there isn't much else for us to say, but...

Hooray for Puzzlooies!
Big fun adventures for you.
Excitement and action
For you to peruse,
With a story in the middle
Of the riddles and clues.

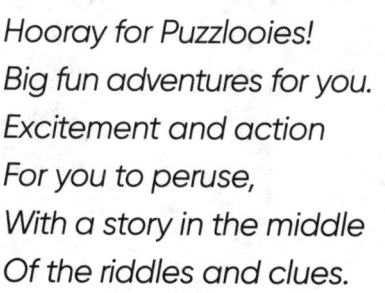

You solved a Puzzlooey.
It's over, it's finished, it's through.
But if a dead famous duck,
Didn't make you say "yuck,"
Another Puzzlooey's waiting for you!

A SOLVE-THE-STORY PUZZLE ADVENTURE

PUZZLOOIES

ONE OF OUR
GIANT ROBOTS
IS MISSING

BY RUSSELL GINNS AND JONATHAN MAIER
ILLUSTRATED BY ANDY NORMAN

For more smart
and silly fun, go to
puzzlooies.com

ANSWERS

ZOO WHO?

1: RAT; 2: PIG; 3: SKUNK;
4: TOAD; 5: WORM; 6: WEASEL

CRACK THE CASE

1 = 20, 2 = 22, 3 = 17, 4 = 21, 5 = 19, 6 = 16,
7 = 10, 8 = 18, 9 = 13, 12 = 23, 14 = 24, 15 = 25.
THE GOOSE EGG AWARD IS IN TROPHY CASE 11!

EGG-ZAMINE IT

1: THE EGG HAS A DENT AND A FEATHER;
2: ONE LEAF IS MISSING;
3: THE STAR IS UPSIDE DOWN;
4: THE MIDDLE OF THE TROPHY HAS A
DIFFERENT SHAPE;
5: THE LABEL HAS ROUND CORNERS;
6: "ACHIEVEMENT" IS MISSPELLED

4 HIGH-WIRE FLIER

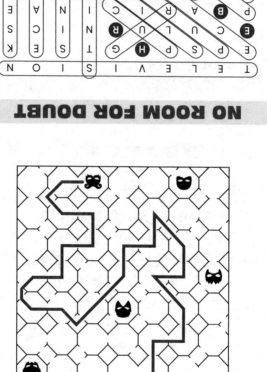

5 NO ROOM FOR DOUBT

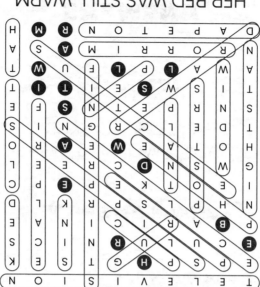

HER BED WAS STILL WARM

A CUT WIRE

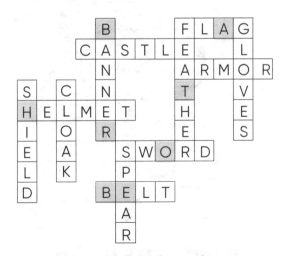

BATHROBE

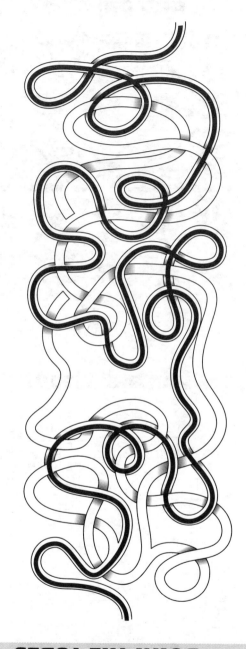

DRAWN INTO DANGER

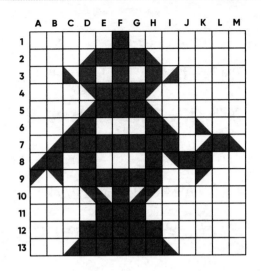

MOVIE MAYHEM

POND WARS THE EMPIRE STRIKES BEAK

BATTLE OF THE BUTTONS

SHUT DOWN

12 ROBOT READOUT

Y	O	U	☺
W	O	N	!
G	O	O	D
☺	B	Y	E

13 FINDERS KEY-PERS

11

14 VIEW KNOW WHO?

MARVIN AND LEWIS

15 DEFACE THE MUSIC

IT SHOULD HAVE BEEN ME

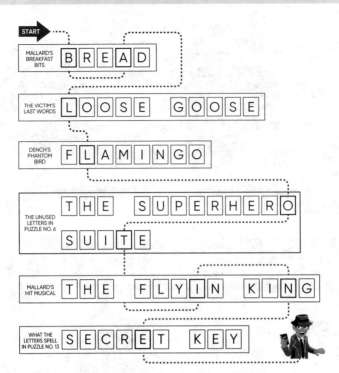

START

MALLARD'S BREAKFAST BITS — B R E A D

THE VICTIM'S LAST WORDS — L O O S E   G O O S E

DENCH'S PHANTOM BIRD — F L A M I N G O

THE UNUSED LETTERS IN PUZZLE NO. 6 — T H E   S U P E R H E R O   S U I T E

MALLARD'S HIT MUSICAL — T H E   F L Y I N   K I N G

WHAT THE LETTERS SPELL IN PUZZLE NO. 13 — S E C R E T   K E Y

BALLOTINE

THEY'RE SMART! THEY'RE FUNNY!
TELL YOUR PARENTS TO
GIVE YOU MONEY FOR MORE...

PUZZLOO!ES

COLLECT THEM ALL!

To learn more about the other zany brainy adventures, visit: